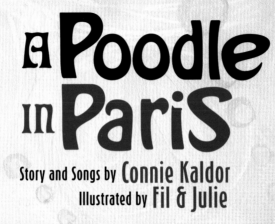

A Poodle in Paris

Story and Songs by **Connie Kaldor**

Illustrated by **Fil & Julie**

Picture a poodle in Paris.
That's the place for a poodle to be.
And the most perfect poodle in Paris
is known as "La Grande Fifi."

If you were to see her,
you'd surely shout out,
"The most wonderful poodle alive!"
If you were to ask her,
"Where is your home?"
She'd stop and say,
"Oh, I have five."

"Five homes," you say. "How can that be?
  One home's enough for most doggies like me."
" *Five homes* is perfect," she'll say with a sigh.
"Come with me through Paris and then you'll know why."

Her first home's a bistro with Madame and Pierre.
She has croissant and chocolate for breakfast down there.
"Oh la la," says Madame as she cuddles Fifi,
while Pierre sings her songs and calls her "ma chérie."

Number two is a shop on the Champs Élysées,
where the finest of dresses are out on display.
Loulou is famous for fashion and style,
and for Fifi, who sits in her window awhile.
Loulou shares her coffee in a tiny white cup.
They've done that since Fifi was
just a small pup.

Loulou

Home three's with the pigeons and Madame Baguette.
By the grand Eiffel Tower is where they all met.
"We love you Fifi," she coos every day,
    "for you never bark meanly or chase us away."

Then there's Rex and there's Charlie, and Collie's one more.
Three friends on a boat that is home number four.
When the Bateau Mouche sails, they all bark at the shore.
Fifi's happy with friends on the river once more.

HOME OF
A GRANDE
FIFI

18

Number five is "Le Bow Wow."
That's easy to see.
There's a sign that says
"HOME OF LA GRANDE FIFI."

"Le Bow Wow" is a club with a Bichon Frise Band
that plays wildly so Fifi can dance the Cancan.
For if you're a dog, there's no greater delight,
than to watch Fifi dance every Saturday night.

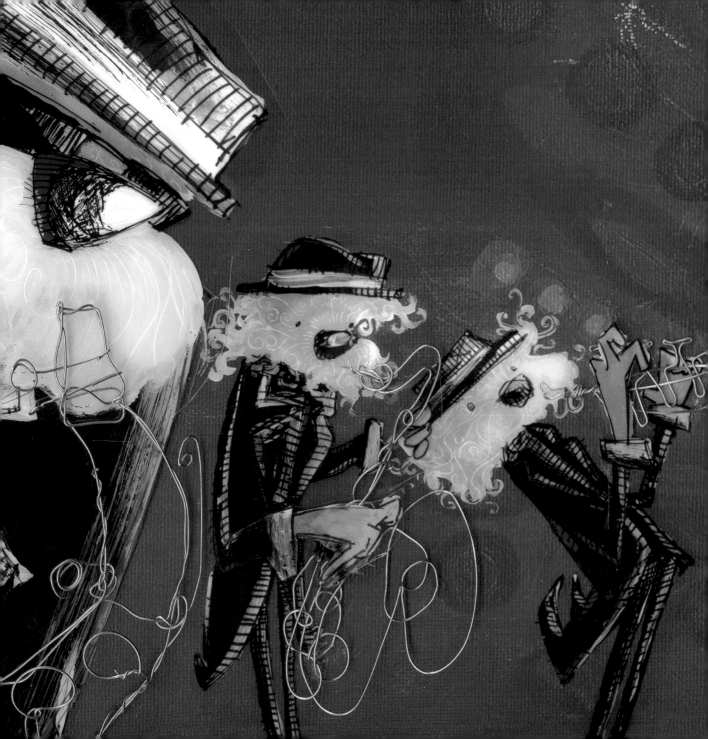

So, if you're ever in Paris and you have the chance
to go out with your dog to watch Ms. Fifi dance,
don't ask about home, for you must understand,
she has one for each finger you have on your hand.

For whether you've one home or five, four or two,
with sisters or brothers or maybe just you,
fancy or plain, bistros or boats,
in the city or out where you find cows and goats...

"Each home is special," says La Grande Fifi.
"I won't part with any place where they love me.
For some dogs stay put, and some dogs will roam,
but where your heart's happy
is where you call home!"

A Poodle in Paris

There once was a poodle from Paris
Of course she called it Paris
This wonderful poodle from Paris
Was known as La Grande Fifi

She had her hair cut just so tied with a purple bow
And every dog that she'd meet would bark and bow
For she danced the Cancan every Saturday night
At a club they call "Le Bow Wow"

Ah Fifi had such flair when she danced to the music
Played by her band of Bichon Frise
And the way she could prance in her Cancan dance
Could bring a Dalmatian to its knees

And every Dashchund and Terrier and Corgi
Would beg for each encore she'd allow
And every Bouvier would fight to get a place Saturday night
At a club they call "Le Bow Wow"

Fifi can Cancan and you can Cancan too
Yes you can Cancan too it's something you can do
Just kick your leg high up in the air kick the other one and there
You can dance the Cancan, you can Cancan too

So if you meet a poodle in Paris
And if she is a beautiful sight
If she seems to say that's my Champs Élysées
Don't doubt for a minute she is right

For she eats croissant and chocolate for breakfast
She drinks coffee in a bowl with a baguette
And she has her way in each sidewalk café
They say ici ma Fifi ma chouette

And if you want to see La Grande Fifi
And know why your puppy would give her all its chow
Just go and see her dance some Saturday night
At a club they call "Le Bow Wow"

Fifi can Cancan and you can Cancan too
Yes you can Cancan too it's something you can do
Just kick your leg high up in the air kick the other one and there
You can dance the Cancan, you can Cancan too

The Littlest Duck

The littlest duck likes to waddle
The littlest duck likes to waddle this way
He goes waddle, waddle, waddle
Waddle, waddle, waddle
Waddle, waddle, waddle all day

The littlest chickie likes to hop
The littlest chickie likes to hop this way
He goes hop, hop, hop
Hop, hop, hop
Hop, hop, hop all day

The littlest fishy likes to swim
The littlest fishy likes to swim this way
She goes swim, swim, swim
Swim, swim, swim, splash
Swim swim, swim all day

The littlest gopher likes to dig
The littlest gopher likes to dig this way
He goes digity, digity, dig
Digity digity, dig
Dig, dig, dig all day

The littlest lark likes to sing
The littlest lark likes to sing this way
She goes tweet, tweet, tweet
Tweedly, tweet, tweet, tweet
Tweet, tweet, tweet all day

The littlest turtle likes to dawdle
The littlest turtle likes to dawdle this way
He goes dawdle, dawdle, dawdle
Dawdle, dawdle, dawdle
Dawdle, dawdle, dawdle all day

Everybody's gotta keep moving
Everybody's gotta move a little each day
You gotta
Waddle, waddle, waddle
Waddle, waddle, waddle, or
Hop, hop, hop
Hop, hop, hop or
Swimmy, swim, swim
Swim, swim, splash or
Digity, digity, dig
Digity, digity, dig or
Tweedly, tweet, tweet, tweet
Tweet, tweet, tweet or
Dawdle, dawdle
Gotta keep moving all day

Betty Is Convinced That She's a Buffalo

Betty is convinced that she's a buffalo
No one can talk her out of this
Right now she is stampeding in the kitchen
She's bellowing and stamping her fist

She's thoroughly convinced that she's a buffalo
That's the way she's acting today
I kinda wish that Betty the buffalo
Was where the deer and antelope play

Now David is convinced that he's a donkey
Just listen to him bray
He says he's only eating alfalfa sprouts
He's stubborn about everything today

He's thoroughly convinced that he's a donkey
A donkey, that's the way it's going to be
I kinda wish that David the donkey
Wasn't such a donkey with me

Now me I'm convinced that I'm a seagull
Even though I haven't wings to fly
'Cause all I want to eat today is garbage
Chocolate bars and deep dish apple pie

I'm thoroughly convinced that I'm a seagull
That's the way I'm acting today
And if I see the Gulf Island ferry
I'm convinced that I will follow it away

The Zoo Was Having a Party

The zoo was having a party
The zoo was having a party
A special birthday party
For each animal there
They invited me to the party
Their special birthday party
I wanted to get a present
For each animal there

What do you get for an armadillo
You better get him a feather pillow
What do you get for a hippopotamus
Well you better get him a lotamus
What do you get for a snake
Well get him a birthday cake
And what do you get for an elephant
Something really swellephant
Something he can smellephant
A bowl full of jellophant
That would be fine
That would be fine

What do you get for a panda
Get him a chair for his veranda
And what do you get for a giraffe
Get him a watermelon cut in half
And what do you get for a whale
Well get him a surfboard and a sail
And what do you get for a monkey
A pet skunkie
Something kinda funkie
A red plastic trunk key
An outfit that is punkie
That would be fine
That would be fine

What do you get for a bear
A bowl of oatmeal and a chair
And what do you get for a flamingo
Get her a game like Bingo
What do you get for a gazelle
Better get him something really swell
What do you get for a baboon
Oh just sing him his favourite tune
What do you get for a gorilla
His favourite ice cream vanilla
His favourite movie Godzilla
Well anything that gives him a thrilla
That would be fine
That would be fine

A Tree Is Just a Tree

Oh a tree is just a tree to you and me
But if you were a blue jay that's not all you'd see
You'd look down on the leaves from way up in the air
And know your nest and family were waiting down there
In that tree, that beautiful tree, that tree

Oh a tree is just a tree to you and me
But if you were a squirrel that's not all you'd see
You'd gather up the acorns and hide them in a tree
And when the winter came around you'd be glad to see
That tree, that beautiful tree, that tree

Oh a tree is just a tree to you and me
But if you were a caterpillar that's not all you'd see
You'd wrap a leaf around your cocoon to keep it dry
A little while later you'd emerge a butterfly
From that tree, that beautiful tree, that tree

Oh a tree is just a tree to you and me
But when the summer sun is hot that's not all you'd see
You'd gladly sit beneath it to cool down in its shade
And that's where you would have your picnic, drink some lemonade
Beneath that tree, that beautiful tree, that tree

Monkeys in the Trees in India

There are monkeys in the trees in India
In India there are monkeys in the trees
And they chatter and they shout
And they scamper all about
And they basically do anything they please

Oh, I'd heard of all the wonders of India
Starting with the India rubber ball
There are camels, tigers, and elephants
But the most wondrous thing of all

No they aren't in a zoo in India
They live all over the place
Underneath the eaves, or underneath some leaves
You can see a monkey's face

They'll dance upon your roof
They'll run along the rails
They'll leap from tree to tree
And they'll swing by their tails

And they basically do anything they please
And thank you

Winners

I think that there should be a hundred winners
It's silly that there is a second place
I think that there should be a bright red ribbon
For everyone who enters in the race

'Cause everyone that joins in is a winner
They all have run the course in their own way
And I think that there should be a hundred winners
So everyone could win a race a day

The only losers are the ones who are standing on the side
They were afraid to enter and they never ever tried
'Cause if you're at the starting line and if you do your best
I think that you're a winner and as good as all the rest

Don't you think that there should be a hundred winners
It's silly that there is a second place
I think that there should be a bright red ribbon
For everyone who enters in the race
'Cause everyone that joins in is a winner
They all have run the course in their own way
And I think that there should be a
Hundred million zillion trillion kinda winners
So everyone would win a race a day
Win a race, win a race, win a race a day

Thelma the Cow

Thelma the cow is singing for you
She sings moo, moo, moo
Thelma the cow is singing the blues
She sings moo, moo, moo

Thelma the cow has fallen in love
And each night she sings to the old moon above
She sings moo, moo, moo
She sings moo, moo, moo
She sings moo, moo, moo, moo, moo

Bozo the dog is singing loud too
He sings awroo, awroo, awroo
Bozo the dog is singing the blues
He sings awroo, awroo, awroo

Bozo the dog has fallen in love
So each night he sings to the old moon above
He sings awroo, awroo, awroo
He sings awroo, awroo, awroo
He sings awroo, awroo, awroo, awroo
Awrooooooooo

Yes Thelma and Bozo are singing for you
They sing moo, awroo, moo
If you have the blues you can sing along too
Just sing moo, awroo, mooo

'Cause you'll never know when you fall in love
And you'll have to sing to the old moon above
You'll sing moo, awroo, moo
You'll sing moo, awroo, moo
You'll sing moo, awroo, moo, moo, moo

Oops Oops Bang Bang

Oops oops bang bang crash bang boom
Something fell over in the living room
I didn't mean it I didn't see
When the table with the vase ran into me

I guess I didn't look where I was going
I might have been going a little fast
Maybe that's why I didn't see
It grab me as I went past

Oops oops bang bang crash bang boom
Something fell over in the dining room
I didn't mean it I didn't see
When the table cloth with the jam and the
milk and that big box of cereal ran into me

Oops oops bang bang crash bang boom
Something fell over in my mom's bedroom
I didn't mean it I didn't see
When the purse with all the powder
and the lipstick and all the perfume in those
kinda broken glass bottles and the papers
and credit cards ran into me

And it seems like all day long no matter what I do
I seem to make a mess of things
in each room I go through
I try to slow right down but every now and then
Just as I am walking slow it happens once again

Oops oops bang bang crash bang boom
Something fell over in my bedroom
I didn't mean it I didn't see

When the pile of all the clothes and the toys and
the stuffed things and oh that big box of Lego with
a thousand pieces that are now under my bed and
I might not ever find them again ran into me

She's My Sister and He's My Brother

She's my sister, and he's my brother
And we belong to one another
When things get rough for one to do
I can count on them to help me through
And they can count on me to help them too

'Cause if I'm bugged by a bully in the schoolyard and
Everybody else is just standing all around
I know they'll leap in and grab that bully by the shirt
And maybe grab him by the leg and yell,
"Teacher, teacher over here" and help me
Bring that bully down

'Cause if they're attacked by old Darth Vader and
Darth Vader sends them out to the middle of space
I know I'm going to leap into my spaceship
And fly all over the universe
Out past the Magellanic clouds
Maybe to another whole galaxy 'cause
No one else could take their place

'Cause if I'm cornered by a real fierce tiger
With a great long tail, big teeth and red tongue
I know they'll grab that tiger by the tail
And swing him round and round and round and round
And swing that tiger to kingdom come

Rubber Boots and Raincoats

Rubber boots and raincoats and big umbrellas
That's what you need in the rain
No use spending the time indoors just
Stuck to the window pane

When you could be out
Splashing about in any puddle nearby
Waiting to see a rainbow
Coming out of the clouds in the sky

Rubber boots and raincoats and big umbrellas

Rubber boots and raincoats and big umbrellas
That's what you need in the rain
No use spending the time indoors
Stuck to the window pane

When you could be out
Playing about with your friends Fred and Stella
Listening to the sound of rain
On your umbrella

Rubber boots and raincoats and big umbrellas

Oh yes, rubber boots, yellow ones and blue ones and red
And all kinds of coats instead
Rubber boots and raincoats and big umbrellas

I Love That Dog

I love that dog
The way he runs up to me when I call
The way he chases his favourite red rubber ball

I love that dog
The way he'll chase his tail all over the place
The way he'll stand up on his hind legs and lick my face
I love that dog

Maybe he is a little bad sometimes
Maybe he barks too loud at night
Maybe he chases cats over the fence
But he's not the kind that growls
And he's not the kind that bites

I love that dog
The way he catches a Frisbee when he leaps
The way his eyes and paws flutter when he sleeps

I love that dog
The way he'll put his wet nose in my hand
And when I tell him my problems he always understands
I love that dog

And on those days when it feels
Like I haven't a friend
He's so glad to see me
That he wags his whole back end

I love that dog
The way he smiles when I pat his head
The way he curls up and snores some nights by my bed
I love that dog
I love that dog

Story, lyrics, music and lead vocal Connie Kaldor Record Producer Paul Campagne Artistic Director Roland Stringer Illustrations Fil & Julie Graphic Design Stéphan Lorti Story editing Mona Cochingyan, Karen Alliston Score Transcription Marc Ouellette Musicians Connie Kaldor piano, acoustic guitar Paul Campagne acoustic, classical and electric guitar, bass, keyboards, mandolin, percussions Davy Gallant drums, percussions, mandolin, dumbek, penny whistle, flute, banjo, electric and acoustic guitar Steve Normandin accordion, piano (The Zoo Was Having a Party, Thelma the Cow) Luigi Alamano trombone, trumpet, euphonium Bill Gossage upright bass Gilles Lauzon saxophone Vocals and vocal effects Paul Campagne A Tree Is Just a Tree, Winners, Thelma the Cow, She's My Sister, He's My Brother Gabriel Campagne Littlest Duck, The Zoo Was Having a Party, A Tree Is Just a Tree, Monkeys in the Trees in India, Winners, Oops Oops Bang Bang, She's My Sister, He's my Brother, Rubber Boots and Raincoats Aleksi Campagne Littlest Duck, The Zoo Was Having a Party, A Tree Is Just a Tree, Monkeys in the Trees in India, Winners, Oops Oops Bang Bang, She's My Sister, He's My Brother, Rubber Boots and Raincoats Luka and Mia Campagne-Gallant A Tree Is Just a Tree, Oops Oops Bang Bang Recorded by Paul Campagne and Davy Gallant at Studio King and Dogger Pond Studio Mixed by Davy Gallant at Dogger Pond Studio Mastered by Renée Marc-Aurèle at SNB
 www.thesecretmountain.com ℗ 2004 Folle Avoine Productions © 2004 Word of Mouth Music and Lac Laplume Music ISBN 2-923163-12-5

Connie Kaldor would like to thank Heather Bishop for singing some of these songs so well over the years, Gabriel and Aleksi for patience, Gilles Losier, Daniel Farra, Karen Bucha, Mr. Frégeau and BDC, the extended Kaldor family, France Allard, and all the wonderful bookstores that opened their doors to the Duck.